ALSO BY HARRY GROOME

Wing Walking

Thirty Below (e-book)

THE GIRL WHO FISHED WITH A WORM

THE GIRL WHO FISHED WITH A WORM

HARRY GROOME

THE
CONNELLY
PRESS

This is a work of fiction. References to real people, events, establishments, corporations, organizations, or locales are intended only to provide a sense of authenticity, and are used fictitiously. All characters, incidents and dialogue are drawn from the author's imagination and are not to be construed as real. Any slights of people or organizations are unintentional.

A slightly different version of this story originally appeared in *Ellery Queen's Mystery Magazine*.

A dollar for every copy sold will be contributed to the Penobscot River Restoration Trust.

Copyright © 2011 by Harry Groome
All rights reserved.

For information about special discounts for bulk purchases, please contact
The Connelly Press, 243 Abrahams Lane
Villanova, PA 19085

Designed by Alan J. Klawans
Composed by Generic Compositors,
Stamford, New York
Printed and bound by Thomson-Shore, Inc.,
Dexter, Michigan

Library of Congress Control Number 2011902591
ISBN 978-0-9797415-2-4
3 5 7 9 8 6 4 2

green press
INITIATIVE

The Connelly Press is committed to preserving ancient forests and natural resources. We elected to print this title on 30% postconsumer recycled paper, processed chlorine-free. As a result, for this printing, we have saved:

2 Trees (40' tall and 6-8" diameter)
654 Gallons of Wastewater
1 million BTUs of Total Energy
42 Pounds of Solid Waste
145 Pounds of Greenhouse Gases

The Connelly Press made this paper choice because our printer, Thomson-Shore, Inc., is a member of Green Press Initiative, a nonprofit program dedicated to supporting authors, publishers, and suppliers in their efforts to reduce their use of fiber obtained from endangered forests.

For more information, visit www.greenpressinitiative.org

Environmental impact estimates were made using the Environmental Defense Paper Calculator. For more information visit: www.edf.org/papercalculator

*With thanks (and apologies) to Stieg Larsson
for giving so many so much enjoyment.*

THE GIRL WHO FISHED WITH A WORM

PROLOGUE

Midsummer Eve, 2009

Olaf Gedda dead? A man with a heart of 24-karat gold murdered?

Gedda was a kind man, a man who wouldn't harm a flea, a man everyone in Sweden knew was rich as a troll, worth close to 60 billion kronor. Often described as one of the big fish in Swedish industry—or as one of the twenty-point stags of the industrial old school—Gedda, as president of the Scandinavian Lunkersklubb, liked being called "the big fish" better. A charismatic man, five feet, six inches tall, who wore his thinning blond hair in a ponytail, at 60 Gedda was a confirmed bachelor who had no one to look after him except his butler of twenty-two years, Henrik Paulsson, and Gotilda Salamander, 26, who had worked for him for three years as his computer expert and, informally, his fishing companion.

What most did not know was that Gedda secretly gave billions each year to hospitals, schools and those less fortunate than he and had littered his will with numerous bequests. *No one* knew, however, that after a snoot full of Skåne Aquavit, he had confided to his lawyer, Manfred von Otter, that when he wasn't fantasizing about catching a trophy trout he fantasized about adopting Salamander, making her the daughter he never had, adding that he frequently dreamt about celebrating her birthday with her each Walpurgis Night.

Von Otter sprayed Gedda with a mouthful of Père Magloire brandy. "Sorry, but you've got to be kidding," he said, nervously brushing brandy from Gedda's jacket. "I thought you were bönking her, not wanting to adopt her."

"Whatever gave you that idea?" Gedda asked. "A little wishful thinking on your part, advokat?"

"No, no," von Otter said, "but I saw her leaving your bedroom—"

"Yes." Gedda smiled a satisfied smile. "Gotilda comes to my room every evening to say goodnight. Sometimes Henrik is there as well. They're like family to me."

Von Otter said he found the discussion educational and again apologized for spitting 21-year-old brandy on his most important client.

The Girl Who Fished with a Worm

One Midsummer Eve—Gedda wasn't sure if it was night or day for at this time of year at latitude 62° north it was light all the time—he was sipping a coffee and reading a book about fly fishing for trout, savoring both his coffee and the book. Written in 1888 by an Englishman named James Tayler and titled, *Red Palmer: A Practical Treatise On Fly Fishing*, Gedda nodded at each of Tayler's thoughts for they seemed to leap from the page like a rainbow trout rising for a Rat-Faced McDougal:

> Everything combines to render fly-fishing the most attractive of all branches of the angler's art. The attempt to capture trout, which are seen to rise to natural flies, is itself an excitement which no other method possesses . . . and, for our own part, we would rather hook, play, and capture a trout of a pound weight with fly, than one of a pound and a half with minnow or worm . . .

"He's right! Goddamned nincompoops with their *jerkbaits* and worms!" Gedda bellowed. "They all should be shot!"

But Olaf Gedda was the one who was shot. On July 4, 2009, he was discovered in his garden in Fiskbenstad, near Hudiksvall and the Ljusnan River, by his butler. He had been killed by a single 124 grain 9mm Makarov bullet that had bored through the corpus callosum and cerebellum of his brain and come to rest in his medulla oblongata.

Other than the bullet and a trowel clutched by Gedda's rigor mortis-stiff hand and a small bucket of worms that lay by his corpse, no other clues were found.

Olaf Gedda's murderer is still at large.

PART 1

Long Odds

*Almost ninety-five percent of
violent crimes in Sweden are never solved.*

Chapter 1

Friday, July 4

Criminal Inspektor Torsten Tonsoffun and his ambitious assistant, Inspektor Nils Noonesson, received the news of Olaf Gedda's murder at the County Criminal Police Violent Crimes Division headquarters in Hudiksvall, near Rosegartan, in the direction of Kyndyrgartån, at 11:47 am. Noonesson walked to the coffee machine and pressed the buttons for two cups while Tonsoffun sat at his desk thinking, Olaf Gedda murdered? This is a big deal; a big fucking deal.

Noonesson placed a coffee in front of Tonsoffun. "I'm having the coroner send the bullet off to NFL by messenger." He paused, hoping that his boss would praise his decisive action. Tonsoffun nodded and signaled for Noonesson to continue. "We should talk to Paulsson to learn how he found Gedda and then talk to the girl, the one that's—"

"Odd as an orangutan at a smörgåsbord?" Tonsoffun asked.

"You took the words right out of my mouth," Noonesson said.

"Okay," Tonsoffun said. "You call the butler; I'll call the girl."

Gotilda Salamander's purple hair was spiked like the fanned crest of a displaying Guianan Cock-of-the-Rock. She had her share of body-piercings too: right ear, one delicate gold ring; left ear, one gold ring and two diamond studs; left eyebrow, a gold stud; nose, a small silver ring; and in her navel, a gold replica of a fish hook while her perfect left breast swelled beneath a colorful tattoo of a #6 Royal Coachman similar in style to the leaping rainbow trout that was the basis for the tramp stamp on the small of her back.

She was working sport gel into her hair and sipping a coffee and smoking a Marlboro Light and admiring the golden hair under her arms when her iPhone 3GS rang. The caller introduced himself as Inspektor Tonsoffun. He had some news for her that he thought would be best delivered in person and asked her to come to police headquarters in Hudiksvall ASAP.

Salamander said she'd be there when the mood struck her.

When she was finished spiking her hair and drinking her coffee, she cinched her black rivet belt above her black chinos, pulled on her mid-length black leather jacket over her tight black T-shirt with **I MEET OR EXCEED EXPECTATIONS** stretched across her breasts in large white type, and stepped out of her apartment at number 19 Iveforgatan. Three members of The Gavleborgs Motorcycle Club stood in a circle around her BMW S1000RR. The one with the most pimples rested his elbows on her motorcycle's saddle. "Well, if it isn't the freakiest fucking chick north of Stockholm," he said.

Salamander seemed to enjoy his comment and smiled her perfect smile. "Get off my bike, you fucking meatball."

"Meatball?" one of the other hoods laughed as he began to circle and taunt her. "What's that all about?"

"We're in Sweden, remember?" Salamander said, and dropped him with a knife hand blow to his temple. Before the second hood could react she blinded him with a two-finger strike to his eyes followed by a *Moorup Cha Ki* to his groin. She watched him collapse on top of his friend and continued to smile at the man leaning on her bike. "And now, how about a *Dwi Cha Gi* to your Adam's apple?"

"A what?" he said, just before she spun and kicked him in the throat with the heel of one of her heavy Doc Marten boots.

Salamander zipped her black leather jacket, mounted her bike and roared east on Route 84, eventually turning west on the E4 just before the Gulf of Bothnia, due west of Kokakola, Finland. When she arrived at the police station, Inspektor Tonsoffun ushered her into his cramped office and shut the door. "Coffee?"

She shook her head.

Tonsoffun invited her to sit, gesturing to one of the two IKEA Verksam swivel chairs in his office.

She shook her head again.

"Fröken Salamander," the inspector began. "I have some very sad and alarming news for you. Are you sure you won't sit?"

She shook her head once more and opened the silver cigarette case Herr Gedda had given her and lit a Marlboro Light.

"Well, alright." He hesitated. "Olaf Gedda was found dead in his garden this morning."

The Girl Who Fished with a Worm

"Dead?" Salamander said. "Papa Gedda?"

Tonsoffun stroked his square jaw with his large right hand. "Murdered."

Surprisingly, Salamander's large blue eyes began to fill with tears—surprisingly, because she never cried. "Who would do such a thing?"

"That's what I wanted to talk to you about. Do you know why anyone might have reason to kill Herr Gedda?"

She sniffled and ran a finger beneath her nose. "Not possibly. He was the kindest, most generous man. He was . . ."

"Was what?" Tonsoffun said.

She wiped her tears from her cheeks. "He was like a father to me."

"I'm sorry," Tonsoffun said. He stared into Salamander's watery blue eyes with his cold blue eyes. "Do I know you from somewhere?"

She shook her head one final time and asked if he was through talking with her. Tonsoffun said yes, but if she could think of anyone who might want to harm Herr Gedda to let him know, and then asked to fingerprint her simply as Violent Crimes Division Procedural Formality 23b.

Chapter 2

Saturday, July 5

Jerker Rhindtwist, publisher and lead investigative reporter of *Umlaut Magazine,* studied the dark roots of his managing editor's dyed blond head as she fumbled with the top button of his Ralph Lauren Slim-Fit chinos when his iPhone 3GS quacked like a duck. He checked to see who was calling, wondered what Inspektor Tonsoffun wanted but didn't wait for him to introduce himself and told him he'd have to call him back.

"I'm afraid this is an emergency," Tonsoffun said. "Your researcher, Fröken Salamander, is in deep doo-doo and you need to talk with her ASAP."

"Umm-hmm," Rhindtwist's editor, Annika Uggla, said as she unzipped his fly.

"Mmm," Rhindtwist muttered.

"Umm-hmm and mmm?" Tonsoffun said. "Listen, Fröken Salamander refuses to speak with a lawyer and I thought maybe she'd talk to you."

"Fine and dandy, but what could be so urgent?"

"We're holding her for the murder of Olaf Gedda."

"Wow!" Rhindtwist tapped Uggla gently on her head and put his hand over the phone. He told her that something else had come up and added, "This could be one hell of a story." He eased out of his chair and lit a Chesterfield. "You've got to be kidding."

"I'm afraid not. We have some very incriminating evidence."

"For example?" Rhindtwist asked in his most penetrating investigative reporter tone of voice.

"Her fingerprints are all over a bucket of worms," Tonsoffun answered.

Rhindtwist laughed. "Your bucket of worms may be nothing more than a *can* of worms."

"Clever," the inspector said. "Only a wordsmith would come to that conclusion."

"Whatever," Rhindtwist said. "Gotilda's played with fire on occasion and even kicked the hornet's nest a time or two, but she wouldn't harm a soul unless provoked."

"Wrong again. She beat the living daylights out of three young men yesterday who are pressing charges for aggravated assault with a deadly weapon."

"Deadly weapon?" Rhindtwist chuckled. "She doesn't carry any weapons. No hammer in her shoulder bag. No Taser. No mace."

"She doesn't have to. She's a fourth dan black belt and technically her hands are lethal weapons."

Rhindtwist said whoever she attacked must have done something to provoke it.

"Maybe. Maybe not," Tonsoffun said, "but she's as nutty as a fruitcake from Åhléns department store, so stop arguing and come up here and talk some sense into her. She's only making things worse for herself by not cooperating."

The inspector's inexplicable sympathy for Salamander and the gravity of her situation weighed on Rhindtwist like a two-and-a-half-ton truck and a twinge of remorse ran through his lanky frame. At one time he and Salamander had been lovers but she had abruptly broken off their relationship and he knew it was he who had screwed things up. Further, he'd dealt with Tonsoffun before and knew he was a good cop—maybe not the sharpest tool in the shed, but a good cop, nonetheless. Finally he said, "Torsten, Gotilda did a short stint of freelance consulting for *Umlaut* a while back but I wouldn't call her a friend, certainly not now. Furthermore, I don't want to get involved with her again. Isn't there someone else who could help her?"

Tonsoffun sighed. "I don't think so, Jerker. I think you're her last, best chance."

"OK," Rhindtwist said. "I'll be there tomorrow but you owe me one."

Chapter 3

Sunday, July 6

Rhindtwist arrived at the County Criminal Police Violent Crimes Division headquarters in Hudiksvall at 10:00 sharp and went directly to Tonsoffun's office where he was introduced to Inspektor Nils Noonesson.

Once they settled in with their coffees, with Noonesson standing because there were only two Verksam chairs from IKEA in the office, Noonesson began the briefing. "First, the bucket of worms that was sitting by Gedda's body has Fröken Salamander's fingerprints all over it. Second, from the angle of the bullet and the lack of powder burns, the experts at forensics say the shooter had to be 5'8" or taller. Third, there is no evidence of a struggle, or that the murderer surprised Gedda, so the odds are it was someone Gedda knew and someone who knew no one else would be around at the time. All three point to the girl."

"Although they could point to others," Rhindtwist said, forcefully.

"Not the bucket with her prints," Noonesson said.

"The bucket could be a red herring to direct you toward the girl," Rhindtwist said.

"Improbable," Noonesson said.

"Any other suspects?" Rhindtwist asked.

"None," Noonesson said.

Tonsoffun shot Noonesson a dark look. "None *right now*, but we should talk with Manfred von Otter, Gedda's lawyer. He knows as much about Gedda's affairs as anyone and may give us some leads. But first, Jerker, can you tell us something about the girl? Her background, what makes her tick. I have a curious feeling—"

"Come on, boss, she's nothing more than a wacko dumb blonde," Noonesson interrupted.

Rhindtwist stared at Noonesson. "Let's get something straight right now. Gotilda worked for me when I was living like a hermit in Thermostådt and I'll agree that at times she's like a hand grenade with its pin pulled, but a wacko—no." He paused to let what he'd said sink in. "When she worked at Handelsbanken, before she struck out on her own, by all accounts they were impressed by her capacity to deal with numbers, computers and her photographic memory. So, Inspektor Noonesson, don't fall into the trap of thinking she's stupid because nothing could be further from the truth."

Noonesson sighed. "So what's with the purple hair and all those rings and studs and not talking to a lawyer, not cooperating?"

"I'm a reporter, not a psychologist," Rhindtwist said, "but I'm sure if you've looked closely you're aware that she could have been a member of our national bikini team."

Both inspectors nodded enthusiastically.

"My theory is that she worries that her beauty and her extreme sexuality diminish her intellect so she's chosen a way to disguise it."

"So?" Noonesson said. "I still think she's guilty."

"Maybe. Maybe not," Tonsoffun said. "Do you know anything about her childhood?"

"Nope," Rhindtwist said. "She never talks about such things."

Salamander was sitting in her seven-by-thirteen-foot cell when Tonsoffun unlocked the cell door and told her that she had a visitor. She curled into a ball on her cot and shoved her hands between her knees. "A visitor?"

Tonsoffun nodded. "Your reporter friend."

Jerker Fucking Rhindtwist. "Tell him I don't want to talk to him."

Tonsoffun lied. "You have no choice, Fröken Salamander. It's a CCPVCD court order."

Salamander said she didn't give a flying fuck if it was by order of His Majesty Carl XVI Gustaf himself; she wouldn't talk with Rhindtwist, no matter what. *Nosey Fucking Pig.*

Tonsoffun stepped into the cell and laid a large hand gently on the girl's shoulder. "Fröken Salamander, please talk with Herr Rhindtwist. You need someone to get you out of this mess and he's your last, best chance."

Last, best chance? Salamander was surprised by her reaction to this authority figure and his plea, and took his hand and pulled herself to her feet. "Okay, Tonsoffun. Five minutes. No more."

Chapter

Monday, July 7

Inspektor Tonsoffun nodded to Manfred von Otter. Gedda's lawyer nodded back.

Tonsoffun turned on his tape recorder. "Monday, July 7, 2009; 0815 hours. VCD confiscation protocol for Olaf Gedda. Library, mahogany desk, bottom drawer. One Jenni Bick leather fly fishing log, one photograph album, size A4, three Manila folders, one marked PERSONAL, one marked WILL, one PARTNERSHIP."

Sipping a fresh cup of coffee, Rhindtwist asked, "What did you learn from von Otter?"

"That your wacky friend stands to inherit 20 billion kronor," Noonesson said. "What more do you need?"

"Some more evidence, Nils," Tonsoffun answered and looked at Rhindtwist. "We confiscated Herr Gedda's legal documents and learned that there are at least two other people who would profit from his death."

Rhindtwist opened a spiral notebook and pulled a BIC Select ballpoint pen from the breast pocket of his denim work shirt that he wore outside his light brown wide wale corduroy trousers from Orvis. "Names?"

"There's really only one," Noonesson said.

Tonsoffun shot Noonesson one of his familiar dark looks. "She's not alone. Paulsson inherits five billion."

"Whoa!" Rhindtwist said.

"Whoa, is right." Tonsoffun said, and went on to say that he'd added Gunnar Håkanson to his list. "Håkanson was Gedda's minority partner. Their partnership agreement states that the business passes to him upon Gedda's death. What's more, he's complained to von Otter on a number of occasions that his 25 percent share didn't fairly represent what he brought to the table."

Rhindtwist wrote three names on his pad, and then a fourth:

Salamander, Paulsson, Håkanson, von Otter.

He punctuated each with a finger on his right hand. "So you've got Salamander, Paulsson and Håkanson. Anyone else?"

Tonsoffun shook his head.

Noonesson shook his head, too. "Get a grip! We've got the murderer locked up. It's an open and shut case."

"I don't think so, Nils," Rhindtwist said, and turned to Tonsoffun. "Mind if I talk with your new suspects and von Otter?"

"Be my guest," Tonsoffun said.

Noonesson shook his head again. "You're wasting your time."

Chapter 5

Tuesday, July 8

At 11:00 the following morning Rhindtwist walked towards Dontgivådamm on Garbogatan, turned up the steep, cobblestone street on his left and climbed until he located 22 Häagen-Dazs where he was greeted by Manfred von Otter who, at six-six, towered over him. Von Otter's greeting was not nearly as intimidating as his physical presence. "Come in," he said, and smiled a toothy smile. "I assume you know that I've told the authorities everything I know and steered them towards all the relevant documents so I hope this is worth your while."

Rhindtwist addressed von Otter formally. "Just a few questions, advokat, for clarification more than anything else."

"It's Manfred, please," von Otter said. "So where should we begin?"

"We could begin with coffee," Rhindtwist said.

"I should have guessed," von Otter said and poured two cups from a thermos carafe on his credenza. Once seated, surrounded on three sides by floor-to-ceiling mahogany shelves filled with books of law, von Otter appeared to feel in charge and asked how he could help.

"I assume you drew up Herr Gedda's will," Rhindtwist said.

"Of course."

"I'm told it includes bequests of 20 billion kronor for Gotilda Salamander and five billion for Henrik Paulsson."

Von Otter sighed. "The girl also gets a life membership in the Scandinavian Lunkersklubb and Henrik gets the small cottage he's lived in for the past twenty or so years." He paused. "May I call you Jerker?"

"Of course."

Von Otter smiled and leaned forward. "Jerker, you must understand that there's a distinction between drawing up a will and counseling a client about its contents." He cocked his head as though he were asking if Rhindtwist understood. "Some of these bequests represented one of many areas in which Olaf and I disagreed, respectfully of course. The most egregious was his gift to that gold-digging girl." He sighed. "I advised against leaving her a cent. Good God, man, what was he thinking leaving her 20 billion kronor? And a membership in the Lunkersklubb? A total sham! The minute Olaf turned his back on her she put down her fly rod and fished with a worm." He drew a breath to compose himself. "The cottage for Henrik was my idea but, even with that, Olaf preferred his overly generous lump sum gift to my suggestion of a modest yearly stipend."

"Hmm." Rhindtwist sipped his coffee. "Sounds like prudent lawyerly advice to me."

A self-satisfied smile crept across von Otter's face.

Rhindtwist asked where the rest of Gedda's fortune would go.

"Olaf never liked to talk about his philanthropic pursuits but the answer is simple: to charities. Twenty-five billion in total. Trout Unlimited will be the primary benefactor with ten billion. But there are many others like Save the Children, Pearl Buck International, Hope 4 Kids International and many small organizations no one's ever heard of."

"He certainly was a generous man," Rhindtwist said, "which takes me back to Paulsson and Salamander. Do you think the butler did it?"

"Certainly not!" von Otter said. "Henrik was very fond of Olaf and wanted for absolutely nothing financially."

"What about his relationship with Salamander?"

Von Otter chuckled. "Let's just say Henrik isn't interested in women, if you know what I mean."

"Hmm. Was he *interested*, as you put it, in Herr Gedda?"

Von Otter chuckled again. "No, but no matter. Olaf was too busy bönking the crazy girl."

"Could Paulsson have been jealous of Salamander?"

Von Otter straightened in his chair. "I strongly doubt it."

"So you've concluded that it must have been Salamander?"

"No question about it."

"You're sure there could be no one else?" Rhindtwist asked. "What about Herr Gedda's business partner? He had a lot to gain from Gedda's death."

"I'm afraid you're grasping at straws, Jerker. Gunnar Håkanson's extremely wealthy in his own right. Besides, he was in Finland when Olaf was murdered. That's where I reached him with the sad news."

"On his mobile?"

Von Otter nodded and asked if there was anything else he could do to help.

"One more question," Rhindtwist said as he stared into his coffee. "Do you own a gun?"

Von Otter appeared hurt by the question. "Jerker, I am a man of the law but, because you asked, yes, I used to own a pistol. It was stolen a couple of years ago. It's a matter of record."

"And you didn't replace it?"

"I abhor any form of violence, especially after what happened to Anna Lindh.* I don't even kill a trout for breakfast anymore and I can assure you *that* takes a lot of self-discipline."

The two men stood and Rhindtwist thanked von Otter for his time. Von Otter in turn offered to do anything he could to help.

---

*Anna Lindh was one of Sweden's most popular politicians, serving as a Member of Parliament, Deputy Mayor of Stockholm, Minister for the Environment and, finally, Minister of Foreign Affairs from 1998–2003 when she was knifed to death while shopping at the Nordiska Kompaniet department store in Stockholm. At the time of her assassination she was not protected by the Swedish Security Service.

Chapter 6

Wednesday, July 9

Rhindtwist fidgeted at his desk at *Umlaut Magazine* and checked his watch. He had an hour before meeting with Paulsson. He walked down Fiskgartan, not far from Kukiejårgatan, crossed Garbogatan and wound his way along the side streets parallel to Woebegatan until he could turn up Anita Ekberg Gata to the Burger King where he ordered a Double Whopper with fries and a Coke Light . . . to go.

A little before 1:00 he parked his silver 2003 Volvo S60 sedan in front of a small thatched-roof cottage that overlooked the Ljusnan River. Henrik Paulsson, a tall, 52-year-old man with a prominent potbelly, stood in the doorway to the cottage and waved at Rhindtwist to come in.

Inside the cottage's small living room Paulsson offered Rhindtwist a seat. Two espressos sat on a silver tray on the coffee table. Paulsson handed one to Rhindtwist and, as he sat, said, "You understand, Herr Rhindtwist, this will be a very unhappy, difficult conversation for me."

"I understand," Rhindtwist said. "Please take your time with my questions. To start, if it's not too difficult, can you tell me about the morning you discovered Herr Gedda?"

"I am a very disciplined man," Paulsson began. "Set in my ways, one might say. I arrive at the mansion house every morning, except Sundays—my day off—at 8:00 to prepare Herr Gedda's breakfast. You can set your watch by it, some have said. On the Friday of the tragedy when I arrived I sensed something was wrong. It took me a moment before I realized that I hadn't been greeted by Herr Gedda's customary, 'That you, Henrik?' and began calling and looking for him. He was nowhere to be seen in the house so I checked the garden..."

Rhindtwist told him to take his time.

"I found him by one of the rose beds." Paulsson began to cry and drew a handkerchief from his pants pocket. "He loved his roses almost as much as he loved his rainbow trout. It was their colors that pleased him so." He wiped his nose and refolded his handkerchief. "I'm sorry. I will get through this." He cleared his throat. "Herr Gedda was laying face down in a pool of blood. I remember thinking it was the same color as his beloved Dusky Maiden roses."

"I know this isn't easy for you, Henrik," Rhindtwist said, "but was Herr Gedda usually out of bed before you arrived?"

"Always. He was what some would call a morning person. It was the happiest time of the day for him. If he didn't go fishing, he read and drank his coffee that I'd set for him the night before or worked in his garden."

"Who else knew of this routine?"

"Everyone close to him." Paulsson smiled. "In his first meeting of the morning Herr Gedda would jokingly boast that while his guests had been sleeping he'd already caught a trout for breakfast or finished a book or clipped a beautiful bouquet of flowers."

"Hmm," Rhindtwist said. "And who was close enough to him to know this?"

"Not that many really. Gotilda, Herr Håkanson and Herr von Otter." Paulsson paused and added, rather proudly, "And, of course, me."

"No one else?"

"I don't think so. You must understand that Herr Gedda was a very private man. Those close to him were like his family."

Rhindtwist was silent for a moment. "Going back to that Friday morning, was there anything odd about how you found Herr Gedda? Did it look like there'd been a struggle or that he'd been surprised by someone?"

Paulsson shook his head. "I can't think of anything but of course I was so shocked by what I'd found..."

Rhindtwist smiled a comforting smile. "I understand, but what about the bucket of worms?"

Paulsson shrugged and looked away.

"Did Herr Gedda often dig in his garden for worms? I thought he was a fly fisherman."

"I'm afraid I can't answer that question."

"But certainly you would have known," Rhindtwist said, sensing that he'd touched upon a nerve.

"It was Gotilda's bucket, not Herr Gedda's," Paulsson mumbled. "I can't add anything more."

"Did she have a routine like yours?"

He nodded. "But she rarely showed up until 10:00 or a little after."

Rhindtwist smiled again to put Paulsson at ease; to have him lower his guard. "Did you hear a shot that morning?"

"I may have, but, as you can see, my cottage is 1,000 meters from the mansion house. The sound I heard could have been a backfire."

"A backfire?"

"When she isn't riding her motorcycle, Gotilda drives to work in an old Volkswagen Beetle that backfires a lot. I thought perhaps she'd arrived early for some reason."

"Hmm," Rhindtwist said. "And was she there when you found Herr Gedda?"

Paulsson sighed. "I can't say for sure."

"So I take it you can't tell the difference between a shot and a backfire?"

"I'm afraid not," Paulsson said. "In this country hunting is the province of the wealthy."

"I understand," Rhindtwist said. "Tell me, what was Herr Gedda's relationship with Gotilda?"

Paulsson flinched. "She took care of his financial and computer tasks and they spent a lot of time fishing together."

"I'm asking if they were romantically involved."

Paulsson stood and moved to the window and looked out over the river. "You'll have to ask her. I was Herr Gedda's butler, not his priest."

"Well put, Henrik," Rhindtwist said. "Only a couple of more questions. Did you know that you were in Herr Gedda's will?"

Paulsson returned to his chair and said he did.

"When did Herr Gedda tell you?"

"He didn't. Herr von Otter did." A dark look crossed Paulsson's face. "He also said that Gotilda is in the will. Is that true?"

Rhindtwist nodded.

"For 20 billion kronor?"

Rhindtwist nodded again. "When did von Otter tell you this? Before or after Herr Gedda was murdered?"

Paulsson put his hand to his mouth and muttered, "Sometime in the spring."

"Do you have any idea why he told you?"

"I think he was, one might say, disappointed that Herr Gedda hadn't followed his advice and was disturbed by the amount Gotilda was to receive." Paulsson leaned back in his chair. "Her membership in the Lunkersklubb bothered him as well. You must understand that Herr von Otter is a purist in every sense of the word. He disapproves of fishing with anything but a fly and suspects that, on occasion, the girl fishes with a worm."

"And how do you feel about all of this?"

"About fishing with a worm? I couldn't care less."

"I understand," Rhindtwist said. "I'm asking about the 20 billion kronor."

Paulsson sighed. "How would you feel? Twenty-two years of loyal service versus her three and she receives quadruple the financial gratitude that I do? It simply isn't fair. There has to be more to it than meets the eye."

"It does raise some questions," Rhindtwist said, and shook Paulsson's hand and said good-bye.

As Rhindtwist walked to his car Paulsson called to him. "I'm only the butler but I watch Inspector Wallander on TV and know that the motive's the thing.

I'd think 20 billion kronor would lead almost anyone astray."

Rhindtwist wanted to tell Paulsson that five billion kronor, damn near 750 million US dollars, wasn't exactly chump change, but he simply waved and climbed into his silver Volvo sedan. With friends like you, Henrik, he thought, Gotilda doesn't stand a chance.

Chapter

Thursday, July 10

Rhindtwist thought it was an interesting turn of the worm that a man of Gunnar Håkanson's eminence would say he planned to be at the Friskis & Svettis gym and could walk over to *Umlaut Magazine*'s office at about 8:30, if that weren't too early. As a result, Rhindtwist and Uggla arrived at 8:00 to make sure coffee was brewing.

At 8:30 sharp an athletically-built man dressed in a shiny navy track suit and wearing a pair of red, white and black Nike Michael Vick trainers pushed open the door on Fiskgartan and called, "Jerker, you here? It's Gunnar."

Not Gunnar Håkanson, just Gunnar. Not Jerker Rhindtwist, just Jerker. Rhindtwist was both surprised and impressed.

Uggla smoothed her skirt over her broad hips, pulled her sweater down to emphasize her perky knöckers and fluffed her dyed blond hair as she hurried to greet their visitor. She introduced herself as the managing editor of *Umlaut Magazine* and her face flushed when Håkanson raised an eyebrow and said, "That's a big job for someone as young as you."

Conveniently she caught one of her high heels in a hole in the carpet and stumbled into his muscular arms. For a moment neither spoke and then Uggla slowly pushed away, her pelvis lingering for a moment against him. Sensing she'd gotten the desired effect she showed him to Rhindtwist's office and, moments later, brought them each a coffee, gave Håkanson a coquettish smile and quietly shut the door behind her as she left.

Håkanson raised his cup as though he were making a toast. "That's one well-built editor you've got there, old sport. Dipping your pen in the old company inkwell, are you?"

Rhindtwist shook his head. "Let's get down to business."

"It's your krona," Håkanson said.

"Let's start with how you learned of Herr Gedda's death."

"I got a call from von Otter."

"Go on."

"What does 'go on' mean?" Håkanson said.

Rhindtwist sighed. "When he called. Where you were. Things like that."

Håkanson sighed. "Manfred called me around noon. He reached me on my mobile in Helsinki. I returned to Stockholm that afternoon." He sipped his coffee and forced a smile. "That's all there is to it."

"How long were you in Helsinki?"

"One night," Håkanson said. "A business quickie."

"Where did you stay?"

Håkanson seemed irritated. "Where I always stay."

"And that would be?"

"That would be the Hotel Kamp," Håkanson said. "You should try it sometime. It's very nice but may be a bit pricey for a journalist."

Rhindtwist smiled a pained smile. "Apparently you're quite a sportsman. Do you hunt and fish?"

"Olaf tried to get me interested in fishing but I'm afraid I don't have the patience for it. I like to go after things, not wait for them to come to me."

"So you hunt?"

"It's a passion of mine," Håkanson said. "Capercaillie and black grouse, as well as elk."

"And you own a gun?"

"Of course."

"Pistols as well as rifles and shotguns?"

Håkanson rocked back and forth in his chair and gave Rhindtwist a disapproving look. "Listen, sport, if you're thinking I was involved in Olaf's murder you're barking up the wrong tree."

"Hmm," Rhindtwist said. "Then what would the right tree be? You stood to gain as much as anyone from Herr Gedda's death."

Håkanson surprised Rhindtwist by saying, "If not more. But as big a pain in the ass as Olaf was at times, he'd been my business partner for over thirty years and, what's more, he was my closest friend. If I've put up with our arrangement for this long, why would I suddenly do something so rash?"

"Greed?"

"Sounds good if you're Shakespeare, who you're not," Håkanson said, "but in real life it's nonsensical because eventually the business will become my family's, no matter what." He stood. "I think we've played this little game long enough. I'd suggest you get your rocks off by bönking your editor, who's as obvious as a mare in heat, and leave the police work up to the professionals because right now it's clear you're in over your head."

"What I do or don't do with Annika is none of your goddamned business," Rhindtwist said. "Now, get the hell out of here."

He watched Håkanson saunter through the office with Uggla following him. He thought their good-byes were inappropriately intimate and drew a coffee from the espresso machine and settled at his desk and buzzed for her. Before he knew it Uggla was standing in the doorway to his office. "What did Gunnar have to say?" she asked.

"Oh, it's Gunnar, is it? Not Herr Håkanson?"

She nodded.

He sighed.

She shrugged.

He lit a Chesterfield.

Finally she asked, "What did you find out?"

Rhindtwist took a drag on his cigarette and slowly exhaled. "Gotilda, Paulsson and your friend Gunnar all had a lot to gain from Gedda's death. On the one hand, both Gotilda and Paulsson got a lot of cash. On the other hand, Håkanson stood to benefit the most because he inherited the business but he has the best alibi: he was in Helsinki when Gedda was murdered. Paulsson doesn't have an alibi and I don't know about Gotilda. Hopefully she'll have a good story. If not, things will get even more difficult for her."

Uggla walked from the doorway and straddled Rhindtwist in his chair. "I think my jealous little boy has forgotten to ask where Håkanson stayed while he was in Helsinki."

Rhindtwist smiled a satisfied smile. "The Hotel Kamp."

Harry Groome

Uggla twisted on his lap and reached for his phone and punched in 00–358–9-42419393. In quick order she was connected with the Hotel Kamp through Helsinki information. "Good morning," she said. "This is Herr Gunnar Håkanson's secretary calling from Stockholm. I'm trying to reconcile his monthly expense report but I'm afraid I've misplaced some of Herr Håkanson's receipts. Could you please give me his charges for . . ." She gave Rhindtwist a questioning look.

He whispered, "Thursday, July the third."

"For July 3 and 4?" Uggla said.

There was a long pause.

"Are you sure?"

Another pause.

"Thank you very much for your trouble." She forced a laugh. "As you can see, I'm lost without my paperwork." Uggla wiggled to face Rhindtwist again. "Well, Håkanson's lying about his whereabouts. The hotel has no record of him staying there this month."

"Hmm," Rhindtwist said. "Good work. Now, what else have I forgotten?"

"Two things." Uggla crossed her arms and pulled her sweater over her head.

Those two? Rhindtwist thought. *Never!*

"First, none of our staff are coming in today and, second, I've locked the door and pulled the shades."

Rhindtwist smiled. He was doing exactly what Håkanson had suggested, only now Håkanson was the prime suspect in the murder of Olaf Gedda. "Hmm," he said, amused that Håkanson thought he was in over his head.

"Umm-hmm," Uggla said as she pulled her skirt to her waist and began to prove, once again, that she was a most excellent choice for Managing Editor.

PART 2

Lumbricus Terrestris

Because they help aerate and enrich the soil, Charles Darwin wrote of earthworms, "It may be doubted whether there are any other animals which have played so important a part in the history of the world, as have these lowly creatures." For this very reason Aristotle called earthworms "the intestines of the soil." They are also frequently called night crawlers because they crawl around at night and angleworms because they make good bait for fishing. They are indigenous to Europe and are hermaphrodites but cannot see or hear. Some have been known to have survived in captivity for 10 years. Neither Darwin nor Aristotle commented on the fact that most fishermen are born honest but get over it pretty quickly whether they fish with a worm, a jerkbait or a fly.

Chapter

Friday, July 11

Salamander drummed her fingers impatiently on the security barrier in front of her as Rhindtwist seated himself. He smiled at her and said, "That color goes well with your purple hair."

Salamander looked down at her DayGlo orange one-piece prison coveralls and said, "Fuck you."

"Well, now that the pleasantries are out of the way," Rhindtwist said, "will you answer some questions for me?"

"It depends on the questions," Salamander said.

"Gotilda, drop the attitude," Rhindtwist said. "And trust me."

"I tried that once, remember? Look where it got me."

Rhindtwist placed a hand on the chainlink window that separated them as though he were trying to touch her. "Please, not now, Gotilda." He sat back in his chair and opened his notebook. "Let's start with your whereabouts the morning Herr Gedda was murdered."

"I was in my apartment getting ready to go to work when Tonsoffun called me and asked me to come up here."

"Was there anybody with you?"

"You asshole. I haven't been with anyone since—"

"My mistake," Rhindtwist said hurriedly. "Any witnesses?"

"That's better." She paused. "No one except the hoods who threatened me outside my apartment."

"And what time was that?"

"Ask Tonsoffun, but I'd say around quarter of ten."

"Problem number one," Rhindtwist said. "The coroner's report indicates that Herr Gedda was killed between 6:00 and 7:00, giving you plenty of time to get back to your apartment and carry on as though nothing had happened."

Salamander gave Rhindtwist an icy stare. "Is that what you think?"

Rhindtwist wasn't sure what he thought but hedged his bets and said it didn't matter. "What counts is that's what the police think, and Paulsson and von Otter think you did it, too."

Salamander felt like a bag of bananas that had been left too long in the sun. "Guilty until proven innocent. I'm fucked."

"Maybe not." He tapped his note book with his pen. "But what's with the bucket of worms?"

Salamander looked down at her hands and twirled her thumbs.

Rhindtwist sensed that, once again, he'd struck a nerve. "Are you keeping something from me?"

"Between you and me?"

He nodded.

She sighed.

He closed his notebook as a gesture of confidentiality.

"I've had a hard time catching a trout with a fly big enough to qualify for the Lunkersklubb so, on occasion," she smiled sheepishly, "I fish with a worm."

"That's it?"

She raised her hands to silence him. "I lost a really good one a few weeks ago—must have been seven pounds—but I know where that bad boy lives and I'll catch him yet."

Rhindtwist was exasperated and confused. "Not if you go to prison you won't."

Glum silence.

Finally, he asked, "Did you know you were in Herr Gedda's will?"

"Of course."

"Of course?"

"He told me."

"When?"

"Some time last year."

Rhindtwist asked if Herr Gedda had told her how much he planned to leave her.

"All he said was that I'd be very comfortable. Von Otter told me about the 20 billion kronor."

"When?"

"A few months ago."

More glum silence.

Rhindtwist opened and closed his notebook. "So, you don't have any witnesses to confirm your whereabouts the morning of the murder and you knew you stood to inherit an obscene amount of money when Herr Gedda died. Both are bad for you. The fact that the murder weapon is nowhere to be found is both good and bad." He sighed. "The bucket of worms could be viewed as a red herring but it also shows that you can be dishonest."

"Me? Dishonest? What about you, Jerköff? You lied to me about Annika when I thought you were finished with her. You left me out in the cold with no family, no nothing, except Papa Gedda, and now he's dead."

"Save that for later," Rhindtwist said. "Right now we've got bigger fish to fry. Unless we come up with something in a hurry you're going to be charged with murder, so think: who might have done it?"

"Could it have been someone who wasn't in the will?" Salamander asked.

"Hmm." Rhindtwist scratched his head. "Maybe, but I don't think so. I've already caught Håkanson in a lie which could prove to be very important."

"Håkanson?" She paused. "Maybe. He's slippery as an eel. When he thought I was bönking Papa Gedda he got really pissed when I wouldn't bönk him. Maybe he was jealous; maybe it was a crime of passion."

"Maybe."

"You're just lucky I didn't kill you," Salamander said.

"Gotilda, please."

"Please, nothing. But I have a question for you."

"Shoot," Rhindtwist said, then hurriedly added, "Sorry."

"Are you still seeing Annika?"

Rhindtwist gave a noncommittal shake of his head.

"Interview's over," Salamander said. She pushed her chair back, stood and walked away. *Jerker Fucking Lying Pig Rhindtwist.*

Chapter

Saturday, July 12

By the weekend Salamander had been officially charged with the murder of Olaf Gedda and Tonsoffun had been ordered to transfer her to the Kronoberg prison in Göteborg on a Saturday when the media would least expect it. He was delighted at the thought of no longer having Salamander as his responsibility even though something about her case didn't feel quite right to him. Putting aside her lack of an alibi and the fortune she stood to inherit and the bucket of worms with her fingerprints, there was something about the girl that made it hard for him to believe she was a murderer. And there was a nagging sense of familiarity he couldn't explain. He sat at his desk sipping his second cup of coffee when

Noonesson knocked on his door. The deputy was giggling when Tonsoffun asked if he was ready.

"In a minute," Noonesson said. He was having a hard time controlling his laughter. "I just heard a new one."

Tonsoffun rolled his eyes. "OK. Then get on with it."

"Here goes," Noonesson said. "Three blondes applied for the job of criminal inspector. They were shown a picture of a suspect by a policeman and asked what struck them most about the photo. The first answered that the man only had one eye. The policeman said that would figure, seeing that the picture was taken in profile. The second blonde said he only had one ear. Again the officer explained that the picture was of the man's profile. The third blonde said the suspect was wearing contact lenses. The policeman checked his file and said she was right and asked how she knew. The blonde said it was simple: with only one eye and one ear how could he wear glasses?"

Tonsoffun shook his head.

"Get it?" Noonesson asked. "With only one eye—"

"For Christ's sake, Nils, I get it!" Tonsoffun said. "Now go get the girl."

Salamander heard Noonesson unlock the outer door to the cell block and immediately felt like a radar installation on high alert. *Inspektor Fucking Noonesson.* She sat on her cot, lowered her head and took a deep breath.

Noonesson unlocked her cell door.

Salamander didn't look up.

Noonesson stepped toward her and said in a sing-song manner, "Time for a change of scene," and freed the handcuffs from his belt.

She extended her hands and then, quick as a lizard, struck Noonesson in the esophagus with a restrained knife hand blow that rendered him speechless and, in the time it takes to say Jack Robinssön, jerked his Sig Sauer P226 9mm pistol from his holster and said, "You make so much as a peep and you're toast."

Noonesson clutched his throat and nodded.

"Now, take off your clothes," Salamander said.

"Huh?"

She waved the Sig Sauer at him. "Your uniform and your shoes and socks. And hurry."

Noonesson stripped to his skivvies and T-shirt and arranged his uniform in a neat pile on the floor.

"Okay, up against the wall." Salamander began to unbutton her prison clothing. "And turn around," she said, as she stripped to her Body by Victoria bra and bikini panties. When she was finished she threw the Day-Glo orange suit at him and told him to put it on, adding, "Let's see how *you* like wearing it, you chauvinist pig." Noonesson turned to pick up the suit. When he caught a glimpse of Salamander wearing only her bra and panties his eyes grew big as saucers.

Salamander watched as he clumsily stepped into the suit and fumbled with each button. When he was through she handcuffed his hands behind him and quickly dressed in his uniform. She turned slowly in a circle and asked in a mocking fashion how she looked.

Noonesson simply shook his head.

"Look, shit for brains," she said, holstering his Sig Sauer P226, "if you keep your motorized mouth shut for five more minutes, everybody's going to be okay." She paused to make sure what she'd said had sunk into his thick skull. "If you can't, things could get pretty ugly."

She locked the cell door and walked purposefully to Tonsoffun's office. Without looking up from his paperwork he asked, "You got the girl?"

Salamander couldn't help but giggle as she pointed the pistol at him. "I'm afraid the girl's got me."

"What the—"

She disarmed Tonsoffun, took away his Nokia mobile phone, Sepura digital radio, expandable baton, keys and pepper spray and handcuffed him and forced him into the cell with his deputy. "Now you boys pay attention," she said. "You've charged the wrong person with Herr Gedda's murder and I'll do everything I can to clear my name." She locked the cell door and walked to the solid steel door that, once bolted, would seal Tonsoffun and Noonesson from the outside world. She turned and said, "I'll call this evening to make sure someone finds you in time for your supper." She reached for the latch on the door and then stared at Noonesson. "Remember this moment the next time you think about telling one of your dumb fucking dumb-blonde jokes. They're not so funny now, are they?" She paused. "Oh, by the way, where are my belongings?"

"In the evidence closet by my desk," Noonesson mumbled.

"That's more like it, inspektor. Thank you." She smiled at Tonsoffun and said, "You take care," and bolted the heavy door behind her.

Once in the office area Salamander fumbled with the keys on Noonesson's large stainless key ring until she found the one she was looking for. The evidence closet was empty, except for her North Face Offsite shoulder bag and a six-pack of Heineken and a stack of *Playboy*s. She unzipped the compartments to her shoulder bag and took a quick inventory: her wallet, her Apple Power Book, her Palm Tungsten T3 and Ericsson T10 mobile were all there.

The Girl Who Fished with a Worm

She piled both sets of keys on Noonesson's desk where they could easily be found and scooped up his car keys and slipped on his Ray-Ban Cockpit glasses. She checked to see if the coast was clear and walked to the white Volvo V70 wagon with its distinctive blue and fluorescent yellow markings that was parked at the side of the station house. She drove slowly south on the E4 turning quickly onto the less trafficked 84 West and soon onto the even more rural 305 North toward Hassela.

A Saab 9-3 Sport Sedan slowed as Salamander drove up behind it. The Saab's left-rear brake light didn't work. Salamander thought for a moment and turned on the cruiser's flashing red light and then hit the siren button, just once, just for the hell of it. The Saab pulled onto the gravel shoulder followed by the Polis car. Salamander pulled her hat low over her eyes and strode confidently to the driver's window. Before she could speak, the driver asked if there was a problem. Salamander said she was driving without a brake light and asked to see her license and registration. Salamander walked back to her car, seated herself and studied the woman's documents.

Click. Ms. Margareta Sörenstam. *Probably single. Probably lives alone.*

Click. Lives at #13 Rottengatan in Hassela. *Just around the corner on Route 307.*

Click. Twenty-two, blonde and 5'11". *Almost my age and height exactly.*

Click. An organ donor. *A caring person.*

Salamander had all she needed. She walked to the passenger's side of the car and tapped on the window. Sörenstam lowered it and Salamander handed back her documents. "Mind if I get in for a moment, Fröken Sörenstam?" she said. "I'd like to ask you a few questions."

The woman nodded and collected a pile of literature from the passenger's seat and tossed it onto the back seat, but not before Salamander could read some of the headings: *Women's Front. The Swedish Federation of Liberal Women.*

Click. A feminist. *My kind of girl!*

Salamander sat and took the keys from the ignition. "Good news, bad news."

"I . . . I don't understand," Sörenstam said.

"The good news is that all you need to do is get your taillight fixed and you won't get a ticket."

"Phew!"

Salamander took off her sun glasses and turned to Sörenstam, her blue eyes bright in the midday sun. She smiled.

Sörenstam smiled back.

"Margareta, the bad news is I'm an escaped convict and stole this uniform and the police car and soon I'll be reported as violent, armed and dangerous."

Sörenstam clutched the steering wheel, her knuckles turning white. "You're not Officer Noonesson?"

Salamander looked down at Noonesson's name badge that was pinned to his uniform blouse. "No, but more bad news/good news: I'm armed but I'm not dangerous, so please try to relax."

Sörenstam hurriedly lowered her window and chucked her cöokies all over the Snow Silver Metallic door panel of her Saab 9–3 Sport Sedan.

Salamander took a Kleenex from a packet on the dash and handed it to her. "If you cooperate with me I promise you won't regret it. I've been falsely charged with the murder of Olaf Gedda and—"

"You? Olaf Gedda? Wow!"

"Wow is right, but I didn't do it. He was like a father to me but nobody believes me."

Sörenstam took a deep breath. She appeared to be regaining her composure. "How do I know you're telling the truth?"

"How do you know I'm not?"

"My father always says actions speak louder than words," Sörenstam answered.

"You're lucky to have a wise father." *Any father at all.* Salamander sat in silence for a moment and then pulled the Sig Sauer from its holster.

Sörenstam raised her hands and cried, "Please don't shoot me. Please don't! Oh, God no, please."

"Margareta, relax," Salamander said, unloading the pistol and handing her the clip of bullets. "Go on. Take it. It's a peace offering."

Sörenstam took the clip and dropped it in her purse as though it might explode in her hand.

Again Salamander smiled. "Now, my name is Gotilda Salamander. The first thing I need to do is get rid of the cruiser and this pig's uniform," Salamander said. "Second, I need to get a wig and some clothes. And I may need you to rent a car for me. How do you feel about all of that?"

Sörenstam was silent.

"Only do it if you want to help. If we're smart nobody will ever know you were involved and I'll be out of your hair by tomorrow."

Sörenstam sat a moment more without speaking and then clenched her fists and banged the steering wheel. "We're kind of like Thelma and Louise, aren't we?" She giggled. "My Pap Pap has an old barn on the other side of Hassela that hasn't been used in years. I know where he keeps the key. We can hide the car there." She paused. "I think we should do that first, Gotilda. Right?"

Salamander smiled. "Right."

The police cruiser and uniform were quickly hidden under lock and key in Sörenstam's grandfather's decrepit barn. Salamander left the Sig Sauer on the front seat but kept the car keys, just in case, and her new identity began to take shape. She removed the stud from her left eyebrow, the ring from her nose, and the replica of a fish hook from her navel, but left the gold rings and diamond studs in her ears before Sörenstam shaved her head down to blonde stubble and bought her a wig that replaced her spiked purple hair with tight blonde curls.

Chapter

Sunday, July 13

At 10:00 the next morning Salamander and Sörenstam drove into Hassela, two young blondes out on a Sunday shopping spree. Their first stop was the 7-Eleven near Tökens Gata towards Tinkersdamm where stacks of *Aftonbladet* sat in the display rack by the entrance, its headline blaring at them:

OLAF GEDDA'S MURDERER ESCAPES

"Holy shit," Sörenstam said. "You're famous!"

"It's only going to get worse," Salamander said. "Next thing you know I'll be on *Sweden's Most Wanted.*"

They bought the newspaper along with a toothbrush, toothpaste, tampons, disposable razors, a carton of Marlboro Lights, eggs, kefir, skim milk, a loaf of whole wheat bread and two coffees and chicken salad sandwiches. Sörenstam paid with her Visa card.

As they strolled down Töotenhattångatan Salamander frequently checked to see if they were being followed. At *Kjol & Blus* she bought two pairs of jeans and *SmartWool* socks, a stylish cloth jacket, Doc Marten boots and a pink T-shirt with **Well-Behaved Women Seldom Make History** written on it. Again, Sörenstam paid with her Visa card.

Their last stop was the Avis office on Route 307 South where Sörenstam leased a Volvo C30 for six months. Once again, she paid with her Visa card. Salamander assured her that she'd pay her back and Sörenstam said that for some reason she knew she would.

Back at Sörenstam's house they quickly unloaded their shopping and huddled close to each other on a small loveseat to read the newspaper:

HUDIKSVALL—A new name and face was added to Sweden's most wanted list today as Gotilda Salamander, charged with the murder of multi-billionaire Olaf Gedda, escaped from the Hudiksvall jail after assaulting one officer and locking him and another in her cell at gun point. That same day Salamander called TV4 at 6 P.M. to say that she was innocent of any wrongdoing and that it was time for someone to go to the jail and give Inspektors Tonsoffun and Noonesson their suppers.

Noonesson said that this type of erratic behavior was typical of Salamander, whom he characterized as "odd as an orangutan at a smörgåsbord," warning that she was armed and considered extremely dangerous.

Police throughout the country are searching for Salamander and the escape vehicle, one of Hudiksvall's two police cars. So far, Noonesson said, the police are clueless.

According to the police blotter, Salamander is 26, five foot ten inches tall with a medium build and spiked purple hair and sports a gold stud in her left eyebrow and small ring in her nose along with numerous piercings in both ears. When she was booked, the police recorded no other identifying marks although it is rumored that the escapee has numerous, colorful tattoos in somewhat intimate places.

Research shows that Salamander was placed in a foster home in Hägersten at an early age but ran away from the home at 13. From 2003 to 2006 she worked in various capacities at Handelsbanken. A spokesperson for the bank said Salamander had an extraordinary capacity to deal with numbers and computers and that many of her colleagues felt she had a photographic memory. The spokesperson volunteered that Salamander had never shown any violent or aggressive tendencies even though she was known to be a serious student of the martial arts.

In 2006 Salamander turned to free-lance consulting, primarily for *Umlaut Magazine*, before going to work full-time for Olaf Gedda.

Gedda was found shot to death in his home in Fiskbenstad on July 4th and, after a thorough police investigation, Salamander was charged with his murder. Gedda's lawyer and close associate, Manfred von Otter, urged that anyone matching Salamander's description be reported to the police immediately.

"You're an orphan?" Sörenstam asked.

Salamander nodded. "My brother and I were separated when we were little tykes. We went to the home but I don't have any idea what happened to him. He just fell off the face of the earth and I've missed him ever since."

Rhindtwist splashed coffee on his GAP Skinny Fit jeans as he bolted upright on his couch. The TV4 Evening News had just been interrupted to announce that a nationwide manhunt was on for Olaf Gedda's murderer. The fugitive was identified as Gotilda Salamander and was reported to be emotionally unstable, armed and extremely dangerous. "Say it isn't so," Rhindtwist said aloud. "Gotilda, please, say it isn't so."

Next a police photo flashed on the screen. Salamander glowered at the camera. Every hair in her purple, spiked comb was clearly visible on his 32" Sony HD Bravia flat-screen, as were the gold stud in her left eyebrow, the silver ring in her nose, and her black lipstick. For the first time Rhindtwist saw Gotilda the way others must see her and shook his head. *No wonder people think she's looney tunes.*

When the report was finished Rhindtwist clicked off the TV and stared at nothing in particular. He found it hard to draw a full breath. His confidence in Gotilda had been shaken to its core. He had thought his investigation of Gunnar Håkanson would eventually identify him as Gedda's murderer but now he wasn't so sure. Now he wondered if all that was said about Gotilda was true. Otherwise, why would she have escaped? He lit a Chesterfield and paced the length of his apartment. He was surprised by the revelation that Gotilda was someone he believed in and wondered what else about her would surprise him. He knew he'd been in love with her once but his inability to say no to Annika's artful and enthusiastic bönking had been the straw that broke the camel's back because Gotilda was an all-or-nothing type of girl. Oddly, Rhindtwist had been successful in suppressing his feelings about her . . . until now. But now regret and remorse came rushing to the surface and he fought the urge to scream that he loved her still but poured himself a fresh cup of coffee instead. As he stared out his apartment window at Sergels Torg he chided himself that he was one fucked-up dude who, on the one hand, thought Gotilda might be a murderer but, on the other hand, might have been his one chance at true love. *Howthefuckdid Igetmyselfintothismess?*

Harry Groome

Inspektor Tonsoffun hunched over his desk studying Sunday's *Aftonbladet*. He couldn't believe what he was reading: "Salamander was placed in a foster home in Hägersten at an early age..." His sister and he had been put in the orphanage in Hägersten in 1985 when she was two and he was four. He was adopted within days but his sister was left behind and he hadn't seen or heard from her since. Was there a chance that Gotilda Salamander, a woman wanted for a front-page murder, was the same girl?

Tips had started to come in from Fiskben and Norrköping and he thought, Jesus, what if some trigger-happy agent from Säpo shoots her? He knowingly violated Violent Crimes Division Procedural Protocol #205 and put out an APB stating that the suspect must be apprehended without excessive force to ensure that a proper confession could be obtained. Tonsoffun was well aware that he would be reprimanded by the County Police Commissioner, maybe even by the brass at SNBP but, frankly, he didn't give a damn.

Chapter 11

Monday, July 14

When Salamander was sure Sörenstam was asleep she left a note on the kitchen table along with 2,000 kronor and a promise to pay her the balance of what she owed her soon. She loaded her shoulder bag into the Volvo and drove along the Norrland coast, eventually turning northwest toward Whatfors until she crossed over the Ljusnan River at the intersection of Route 84. Here she pulled off to the side of the road and walked back to the bridge. It was 2:15 Monday morning. *Ten days since Papa Gedda was killed. Ten days of hell, of confusing time with Jerker Rhindtwist.*

She studied the river, debating if she should look upstream to see what life was going to bring her, or look downstream to see what had passed her by, what she was leaving behind. She elected to watch the river glide toward her, wondering if the answer of what was next lay beneath its broken surface. She lit a cigarette and lingered for a moment and then hurried to her car and drove until she found the unmarked dirt road that led to the cottage where she and Papa Gedda, and on occasion Manfred von Otter, had spent many a weekend fishing for trout—the cottage that would be her secret headquarters until she proved her innocence.

Rhindtwist sat at his kitchen table drinking his first coffee of the day and smoking a Chesterfield. He opened his old Macintosh PowerPC with a hard disk of only 750 MB. He went to **[New Mail]** and choked as he inhaled because the first message was from: <rainbowlady@hotmail.com>.

i need håkanson's e-mail address. sorry . . .

Rhindtwist scrolled through his **[Address Book]** and hit **[Reply]**.

The Girl Who Fished with a Worm

<u>gunhak41@global.com</u>. **r u ok? how can i help? b friendly, please.**

He waited less than a minute for Salamander's reply:

all OK. more when i'm ready. don't push it . . .

Well at least she's OK. He smiled. And she thinks it's Håkanson, too. "Of course she's innocent," he said out loud, "and I hope she nails that bastard. Please, God, don't let her fail."

Salamander balanced her G4 titanium seventeen-inch Apple Power Book on her lap, opened Asphyxia 1.3 and entered *honeybee* as her ID and *MickeyFinn10* as her password. Within minutes she was into the mirrored hard drive of Håkanson's laptop. A feeling of relief, then victory and, finally, satisfaction came over her. *I'm home. In my secret world of discovery. In someone else's private life. And he has no idea I'm here. If only it were this easy with Jerker Fucking Rhindtwist.*

69

Salamander scrolled through Håkanson's e-mail, starting July 1. A message to <VanessaLindgren@aol.com> on July 3 caught her eye:

The Sheraton at seven. Room 411. Wear that low-cut black number with no back.

Salamander continued to search. On July 4 at 12:05 pm Håkanson wrote Vanessa Lindgren again:

Can't do our afternoon thing. Manfred just called to tell me that Olaf was murdered this morning. I lied and told him I was in Helsinki and would be back ASAP. I can't quite believe the news. Olaf has been such an important part of my life and not just as a business partner but as a loyal friend. I don't know what I'll do without him. I'm very, very sad. Please say a prayer for him. I'll be in touch. How could this have happened?

Salamander found a message on July 11 to: <Editor Uggla@umlaut.com.>

Thinking of you. Could we meet?

Salamander shook her head. *That creep!*

Uggla answered:

Thinking of you, too. Some night after work?

Tonight? 7:00 at Café Hedon?

The Sheraton's closer.

I'll take the tunnelbana.

Will you get a room?
Yes, and I'm getting a böner.
That's the whole point!

Salamander called the Sheraton to verify that Håkanson had spent the night of July 3 and then started up the ICQ chat programme and pinged up the address she'd created for Rhindtwist through the Yahoo group **[Idiot's-Delight]**.

<I've got news.>

<Talk to me.>

<You men and your nöokie. Håkanson wasn't in Helsinki, he was at the Sheraton with some bitch in a black dress.>

<He still had time to kill Gedda.>

<His e-mails strongly suggest he didn't.>

Rhindtwist sighed. **<That leaves Paulsson.>**

<Hard to believe. We need the gun or something.>

<Anything more?>

<You're not going to like it. Håkanson's bönking Annika too.>

<No time for jokes.>

<No joke. She's even hornier than you. Maybe it's your wake up call.>

<Touché.>

Salamander laughed out loud for the first time in weeks and signed off.

PART 3

A Needle In A Haystack

Reportedly, there are 155,000 handguns in civilian possession in Sweden.

Chapter

Tuesday, July 15

*P*aulsson *the only suspect? NFW.* Salamander thought spending a little time fishing might clear her head. She filled a thermos with coffee, grabbed her tackle box, a small Tupperware container filled with night crawlers, her Winston Boron II fly rod and her Ugly Stik® and hiked along the bank of the Ljusnan to the deep pool where she'd lost a large trout earlier in the season.

Three trout rose throughout the pool. Salamander sprayed herself with 100% DEET to ward off Whatfors' notorious mosquitoes and cast, her cream-colored dry fly settling delicately on the water. On her fourth cast she caught a 9" brown trout and gently released it. Within fifteen minutes she caught and released two more, the largest 13" long.

She sat on the bank, poured herself a coffee, smoked a cigarette, and waited for other fish to show. She stared at the rushing water and listened to its song. She wasn't sure how she'd gotten herself into this mess and was even less sure how she'd get out of it when a large trout porpoised at the head of the pool.

She cast a March Brown, a Quill Gordon, an Au Sable Wulff and a Cinnamon Ant to the fish without any success. *Ahwhatthehell.* She picked up her spinning rod, threaded a worm on its treble hook and cast. The worm grazed the rocks at the head of the pool and sank slowly. Salamander scraped and bounced it along the bottom. Suddenly it stopped. She waited and reeled a bit more. Her line tightened and her rod bowed. She reeled again, expecting the trout to run and try to wrap her line around a log or a rock, but it simply sat and sulked. She thought it must be one big fucking brownie. She reeled slowly until she could see it, dark and motionless, and then realized it wasn't a fish, and hurriedly reeled whatever it was to her. *Oh my God, it's a gun!* Her treble hook had snagged a pistol by its trigger guard. She dropped it into her net, snipped her line, gathered her gear and rushed back to the cottage to make some sense out of what had just happened.

The Girl Who Fished with a Worm

She laid the pistol on a towel and signed into Asphyxia 1.3 and navigated her way to the hard drive of SNBP's mainframe. She typed in **[firearms registration]**, clicked on **[Search]** and entered the pistol's make, model and serial number. **[Not found]** She typed in **[missing weapons]** and retyped the details. Her screen went blank and then reported: **[Polish P-83 Wanad, 61068798, reported stolen 2007-06-22, Manfred von Otter, 22 Häagen-Dazs, Stockholm 111 43]**

Advokat Bastard von Otter!

She reopened Asphyxia 1.3 and hacked her way into von Otter's system. Folder after folder was in a lawyerly order. She opened **<Olaf Gedda's will>** and slogged through the legal bullshit stopping at the list of beneficiaries: Paulsson and herself, a few well-known charities such as Trout Unlimited and Pearl S. Buck International, and a much longer list of organizations she'd never heard of. Out of curiosity she picked *Worldwide Daycare*, earmarked for one billion kronor, and Googled it. *KinderCare* topped the list. No *Worldwide Daycare*.

Salamander Googled a second one billion kronor beneficiary, *Help Homeless Haitians. UNICEF,* and *USAID* came up, but no *Help Homeless Haitians*. She opened a Word document titled **[Help Homeless Haitians]**. The content was short and sweet. **[Deposit**

one billion kronor in Barclays Bank PLC, Account No. 40408743.]

She opened **[Worldwide Daycare]**. Same instructions, same Barclays' account number.

How did that son of a bitch get Papa Gedda to sign this? Well, Advokat Fucking von Otter, no catch and release for you!

Rhindtwist was preoccupied by the deadline for the upcoming issue of *Umlaut* when his iPhone quacked like a duck. He sighed. It was Tonsoffun.

"I'll be quick," Tonsoffun said. "Have you heard from the girl?"

"No."

"I don't believe you, but OK." Tonsoffun paused. "Jerker, man to man?"

Rhindtwist scowled and said, "Man to man."

"At one time Gotilda and you were intimate."

"Intimate?"

"You were sleeping with her, right?"

"Jesus, Torsten, what's with you and Noonesson and your sexual fantasies?"

"Cool it," Tonsoffun said. "Does she have a strawberry birthmark on her lower back?"

Rhindtwist sat stock-still and stared at his mobile. *Howinthehelldoesheknowthat?* He lit a Chesterfield and nodded as though Tonsoffun could see him. "Yes, but she covered it with a tattoo of a rainbow trout." He heard Tonsoffun begin to sob when his ICQ pinged. **<I've got our man.>** "I'll call you right back," he said to Tonsoffun, and hung up.

<Who?>

<Von Otter.>

<You sure?>

<99%. We need a ballistics check.>

<You have the weapon?>

Salamander took a picture of the pistol with her iPhone.

<Check your e-mail.J>

Her message contained a JPEG. He double-clicked and opened Photoshop.

<How did you get it?>

<It's a long story. Meet me at Papa Gedda's fishing cottage ASAP but no police. Not yet.>

Rhindtwist waved at his managing editor on his way out of the office. "You're in charge, Annika. Make sure it's a great issue. That's why I hired you." That, he thought, and for your other obvious assets; but those days have come to an end. He chuckled and muttered in English, "Been there. Done that. Bought the T-shirt."

On his drive north he called Tonsoffun and asked how he knew about Gotilda's birthmark. When he answered, "She's my sister," Rhindtwist almost drove his Volvo S60 sedan into the guardrail on the E4. Once he pulled himself together and Tonsoffun had told him his story, he comforted the inspector by telling him to relax, that Gotilda and he would be happily reunited soon.

Rhindtwist arrived at the cottage to find Salamander eating pickled herring and deer stew and drinking a Vestfyn Pilsner. Without saying hello she held up a Ziploc bag containing the P-83 Wanad. "That should do it."

"Please explain."

She didn't tell him she hooked the pistol while fishing with a worm. Instead she said she found it in the shallow riffle at the tail of the pool.

"What more?"

She took him through the results of her computer hacking and von Otter's creation of phony charities. "If that's the murder weapon, the case is closed."

Rhindtwist pointed to the Jura Impressa X7 espresso machine behind her and asked if he could have a cup.

She nodded.

The Girl Who Fished with a Worm

He poured a coffee and lit a Chesterfield. "So that's it?"

Salamander shrugged. "What's to add?"

"What about you and me? Case closed there, too?"

She lit a Marlboro Light and smoked it without speaking. Finally she said, "You want a second or third or fourth chance?"

"Look, I didn't give up on you with this Gedda thing and I'm through with Annika. So, yes, I'm asking for one last chance."

Salamander pushed the plastic bag with the weapon in it toward him. "Get this to the National Forensics Laboratory ASAP and . . ."

"And what?"

"And I'll think about us."

Chapter

Friday, July 18

Rhindtwist arrived at Gedda's mansion ahead of the police. Von Otter was waiting for him and gave him a toothy smile. "Nice to see you, Jerker."

"Thanks for agreeing to meet with me," Rhindtwist said, and suggested they take a walk.

As they strolled through the rose gardens von Otter asked, "Have they found the girl?"

Rhindtwist said, "No."

Von Otter said, "Pity."

"But they have found the murder weapon."

Von Otter straightened to his full six foot six. "That's hard to believe."

"What's harder to believe is that the Wanad belonged to you."

Von Otter's calm expression never changed. "I knew Salamander had stolen it. I knew it!"

Rhindtwist saw he'd taken the bait and said, "That explains that."

Von Otter nodded confidently. "That explains that."

Rhindtwist stopped walking and took him by the arm. "So how do you explain all the phony charities in Herr Gedda's will that directed their donations to your account at Barclays?" Von Otter jerked free from his grip but Rhindtwist simply smiled and said, "There's no place to run, Manfred. The police are on their way."

Von Otter sighed. "But how?"

"Better yet, why?" Rhindtwist asked.

Von Otter began to tremble. "That bastard Olaf refused me membership in the Lunkersklubb, said I hadn't earned it even though I'd caught a six pound rainbow a few years ago. And then he gave a *life* membership to that worm-fishing little whore? Unfair! But that was just the beginning. He wouldn't listen to me about the will and left her 20 billion kronor. Twenty billion! And five billion to Henrik not to mention the goddamned cottage—*my* idea, mind you—but not a krona to me!" He paused and muttered, "And after all I'd done for him."

"So you planted the bucket of worms to implicate the girl."

Von Otter nodded. "That, and to let the whole world know that when it came to fishing she got away with murder there, too."

"Hmm," Rhindtwist said, and took von Otter by the arm again and began to lead him back to the house. As they passed the rose bed where Gedda had been found von Otter stopped and began to cry. "Forgive me, Olaf. Please forgive me."

When they reached the terrace that overlooked the river they sat without speaking. Finally, von Otter wiped his tears and broke the silence. "I'll have you know, I wasn't alone. Henrik was involved."

"Go on."

"One night, after Olaf had had one too many Aquavits, Henrik went to his room to say goodnight and asked him to sign revised copies of his will, saying that I'd found some typos in the originals. What Olaf signed contained what you refer to as the 'phony charities.'"

"And in return for Henrik's help you did the dirty work for him."

"Precisely."

As von Otter spoke Rhindtwist heard footsteps behind him. He turned slowly to see Paulsson pointing Gedda's prized Purdey double-barreled shotgun at him. "Manfred, you talk too much," Paulsson said, "and you've left me no choice. But, if I do this correctly, it will look as though you killed Rhindtwist when he confronted you and I disarmed you and had no choice but to kill you in self-defense." He walked between the two men and leveled the gun at Rhindtwist. "Clever for a domestic, no?"

The click of Paulsson pushing off the safety was drowned out by a bloodcurdling *"Ki Hap!"* as Salamander leapt over a wicker Pottery Barn all-weather chaise and snap-kicked the gun from Paulsson's hands with an *Ahp Cha Nut Gi* followed by a jump spinning back kick to his esophagus with the heel of one of her new Doc Marten boots. Paulsson dropped to the terrace, choking and grabbing at his throat, and then she immobilized him with a low reverse punch to his temple.

"Wow!" a voice said.

Von Otter grabbed for the shotgun but Salamander kicked it out of his reach, sending it scraping and spinning across the flagstones. She smiled at him and said, "Payback time, asshole. For Papa Gedda. For fucking up my life."

He turned tail to run but Salamander stopped him with a low-high roundhouse kick, first to his kidneys, then to his jaw. She smiled again at the immobile giant and delivered a *Moorup Cha Ki* to his groin that doubled him over screaming with pain, the sound giving her immense satisfaction, and then she used a downward elbow strike to the base of his skull to splay him motionless on the terrace.

"Holy shit!" the voice said.

Salamander turned. Inspektor Noonesson stood in the doorway, dumbfounded. He shook his head and said, "I take it all back, Fröken Salamander. All of it."

From behind her she heard another familiar voice say, "Nils, handcuff Paulsson if you wouldn't mind." Inspektor Tonsoffun was kneeling by von Otter's prone body handcuffing him. When he was through he stood and placed his large hands on Salamander's shoulders. His blue eyes were filled with tears. "Are you OK, Tillie?" he asked.

Salamander gave him an odd look. Tillie was the nickname she'd been given in the foster home in Hägersten. The comfort of Tonsoffun's touch also confused her. "I don't get it," she said.

He smiled through his tears. "I'm not just Criminal Inspektor Torsten Tonsoffun, Tillie. I'm *your* Torsten. Your brother."

Salamander pulled him to her and said, "At last," and they both began to sob with joy.

Once Paulsson and von Otter were able to stand, Tonsoffun and Noonesson ushered them to their cruiser and shoved them into the back seat. "Wait. I forgot," Salamander said and handed Noonesson the keys to the car she'd stolen along with neatly written instructions on where he'd find it. "Your pistol's on the front seat."

Once again Noonesson shook his head.

The Girl Who Fished with a Worm

Salamander smiled for the third time that morning. "Not bad for a dumb blonde, eh Nils?"

Noonesson saluted. "Not bad at all."

Salamander kissed her brother good-bye and said she'd see him tomorrow. She watched the cruiser disappear down Papa Gedda's long driveway when Rhindtwist asked, "How about a coffee?"

Gotilda patted his arm, the first time she'd touched him in over two years, and smiled through her tears. "Why not, Jerker? We're in Sweden, remember?"

SKÅL

Thanks to the following:

The eagle-eyed Millers, Edward and Dottie (not related, or, if they are, they won't admit it), for checking every umlaut to make sure all was hunky-döry.

Noomi Rapace for putting a little more spring in the step of girls throughout the world and for her frequent phone calls asking if she could play Gotilda in the soon-to-be-major motion picture.

Elite hacker Kevin Brown for guiding Gotilda through Asphyxia 1.3 and other mysterious computer-type stuff.

Nora Ephron who provided shouts and murmurs of inspiration above and beyond "THE GIRL WHO FIXED THE UMLAUT."

Janet Hutchings, editor of *Ellery Queen Mystery Magazine*—"The World's Leading Mystery Magazine"—for her vote of confidence and the editors of *Worm Fishing Weekly* for their smashing review.

And, finally, His Majesty Carl XVI Gustaf, The King of Sweden, for encouraging me to write this when others were skeptical (to say the least).

ABOUT THE AUTHOR

Harry Groome's writings have appeared in dozens of magazines including *Gray's Sporting Journal, Ellery Queen Mystery Magazine, Aethlon: The Journal of Sport Literature* and *Field & Stream*. Harry has an MFA in writing from the Vermont College of Fine Arts and is a fly fisherman who never admits to fishing with a worm.

Visit Harry's website at www.**harrygroome.com**

ABOUT THE TYPE

The Girl Who Fished With A Worm was set in Palatino Linotype.

The Linotype machine was invented by Ottmar Mergenthaler in 1884. It produces an entire line of metal type at once (hence a *line-o'-type*) allowing for much faster typesetting and composition than original hand composition in which operators placed down one pre-cast metal letter at a time. Major newspaper publishers retired Linotype and similar "hot metal" typesetting machines during the 1970s and 1980s, replacing them with photo-typesetting equipment and, later, computerized typesetting.

Palatino is a large typeface family designed by Hermann Zapf in 1948. Named after 16th century Italian master of calligraphy, Giambattista Palatino, the typeface is based on the humanist fonts of the Italian Renaissance which mirror the letters formed by a broad nib pen, giving it a calligraphic grace and

Harry Groome

making it easy to read. In 1999 Zapf revised Palatino for Linotype and Microsoft. The revised typeface incorporates extended Latin, Greek, and Cyrillic character sets and is one of the few fonts to incorporate an interrobang‽